A Gift For:

From:

Published by Hallmark Books,
a division of Hallmark Cards, Inc.,
Kansas City, MO 64141
Visit us on the Web at www.Hallmark.com.

Art Director: Kevin Swanson
Production Artist: Dan Horton

ISBN: 978-1-59530-335-6

BOK6182

Printed and bound in China
DEC10

silly jilly's
specquackular
day

By Chelsea Fogleman
Illustrated by Jeanne Rittmueller

Jilly was a little duck who loved big adventure.

One spring morning, she was waddling along and heard a country bird talking to a small piglet. "There is a magical place where bread falls from the sky . . ."

Jilly stopped dead in her tracks. (She couldn't help listening—bread was her favorite thing in the whole wide world!)

The tiny piglet drooled. "Bread falls from the sky?" he squeaked.

"That's right," answered the country bird. "It lands in the water on the other side of the pond."

"Awww," the piglet snorted. "I can't go in the pond. I don't know how to swim."

Jilly's little heart pounded. She could swim! In fact, she was a very good swimmer. Maybe she could find the magical place where bread fell from the sky!

"I could leave now and still be back for my quacking lesson with Mama Duck," she realized.

Suddenly determined, Jilly shuffled her feet toward the nearest shore. She hopped in the water with a splash.

It wasn't long before Jilly was feeling quite happy. It was a bright, sunny day. Birds chirped, bugs buzzed, and flowers bloomed everywhere.

When she had been floating for a while, Jilly began to think, "I must be getting close now." She stretched her neck to look ahead. Then her small eyes grew humongous. "Uh-oh," she said.

A thick patch of reeds was blocking Jilly's path! There was no way to swim around it—she would have to go through it.

This was more than a teensy-weensy problem, because the reeds would certainly tickle.

And if Jilly was anything, she was very . . . very . . . VERY ticklish.

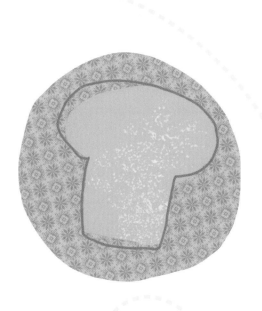

Jilly thought about turning back, but bread was at stake. (Maybe it would even be a little stale, the way she liked it most.)

Looking ahead, Jilly cried at last, "Oh, I can't let some silly reeds stand in my way." So she swam onward with her bill held high.

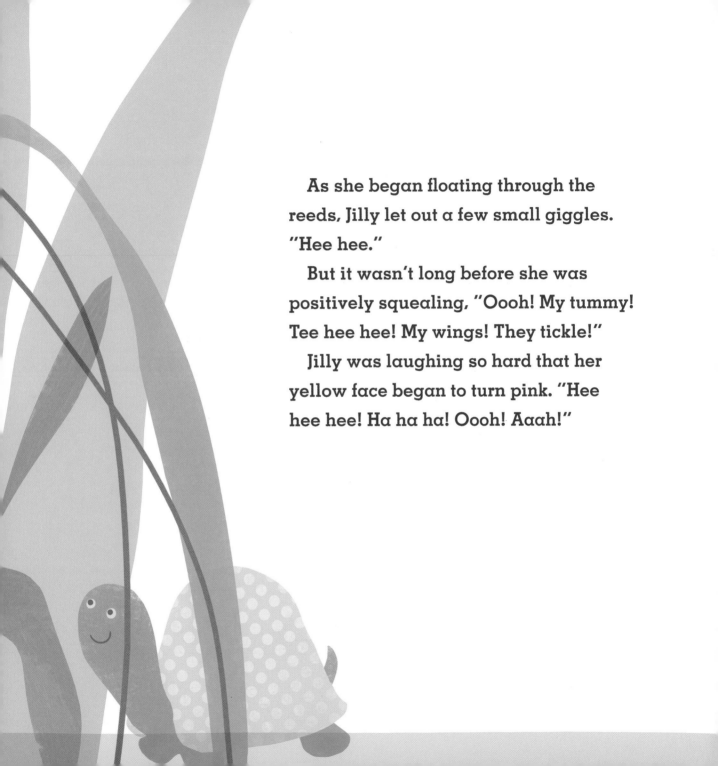

As she began floating through the reeds, Jilly let out a few small giggles. "Hee hee."

But it wasn't long before she was positively squealing, "Oooh! My tummy! Tee hee hee! My wings! They tickle!"

Jilly was laughing so hard that her yellow face began to turn pink. "Hee hee hee! Ha ha ha! Oooh! Aaah!"

By now, Jilly couldn't stop wiggling, wriggling, and giggling! Her wings flapped harder and harder until something amazing happened . . .

Suddenly the reeds weren't tickling her anymore. Surprised, she looked down and gasped. "I'm flying!"

Jilly had flapped her wings so hard that she had lifted herself into the air!

With wings still beating, Jilly began to look around.
Now she could easily see the other side of the pond. "I
can fly there," she said, puffing up her feathers. Then
she proudly glided over the rest of the pesky reeds.

"Ahhh!" She smiled as she plopped into the water
near shore.

Jilly was so excited about flying that she almost forgot why she had crossed the pond at all.

Then her tummy growled. *Grrr.*

"Well, now that I'm here," she breathed, "bread should be falling from the sky." She gazed up and saw only blue sky and giant marshmallowy clouds.

Jilly was disappointed. Her neck drooped. Maybe the country bird had been wrong. Maybe bread didn't really fall from the sky on this side of the pond.

Then something tapped her wing . . .

A small white crumb was bobbing in the water right
beside Jilly. "There you go, ducky!" someone called out.
Jilly looked up. There were children throwing bread into
the water. They were feeding the ducks and fishies!

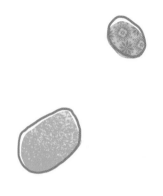

Jilly gobbled up the soggy morsel and happily shook her tail feathers. "Yum! Yum!" she squawked. "What a specquackular day!"

Did this book tickle you silly
and fill the duck bill?
We would love to hear from you!

Please send your comments to:
Hallmark Book Feedback
P.O. Box 419034
Mail Drop 215
Kansas City, MO 64141

Or e-mail us at:
booknotes@hallmark.com